ANIMALS OF THE FOREST

Raccoons

by Al Albertson

BLASTOFF! READERS 2

BELLWETHER MEDIA • MINNEAPOLIS, MN

Note to Librarians, Teachers, and Parents:

Blastoff! Readers are carefully developed by literacy experts and combine standards-based content with developmentally appropriate text.

Level 1 provides the most support through repetition of high-frequency words, light text, predictable sentence patterns, and strong visual support.

Level 2 offers early readers a bit more challenge through varied simple sentences, increased text load, and less repetition of high-frequency words.

Level 3 advances early-fluent readers toward fluency through increased text and concept load, less reliance on visuals, longer sentences, and more literary language.

Level 4 builds reading stamina by providing more text per page, increased use of punctuation, greater variation in sentence patterns, and increasingly challenging vocabulary.

Level 5 encourages children to move from "learning to read" to "reading to learn" by providing even more text, varied writing styles, and less familiar topics.

Whichever book is right for your reader, Blastoff! Readers are the perfect books to build confidence and encourage a love of reading that will last a lifetime!

This edition first published in 2020 by Bellwether Media, Inc.

Library of Congress Cataloging-in-Publication Data

Names: Albertson, Al, author.
Title: Raccoons / by Al Albertson.
Description: Minneapolis, MN : Bellwether Media, Inc., 2020. | Series: Blastoff! readers: animals of the forest | Includes bibliographical references and index. | Audience: Ages 5-8 | Audience: Grades K-1 | Summary: "Relevant images match informative text in this introduction to raccoons. Intended for students in kindergarten through third grade"-- Provided by publisher.
Identifiers: LCCN 2019024603 (print) | LCCN 2019024604 (ebook) | ISBN 9781644871294 (library binding) | ISBN 9781618918055 (ebook)
Subjects: LCSH: Raccoon--Juvenile literature.
Classification: LCC QL737.C26 A43 2020 (print) | LCC QL737.C26 (ebook) | DDC 599.76/32--dc23
LC record available at https://lccn.loc.gov/2019024603
LC ebook record available at https://lccn.loc.gov/2019024604

Editor: Betsy Rathburn Designer: Josh Brink

Printed in the United States of America, North Mankato, MN.

Table of Contents

Life in the Forest

Raccoons are small and furry **mammals**. They are known for their ringed tails!

Raccoons have **adapted** to many places. But most **thrive** in the forest **biome**.

Northern Raccoon Range

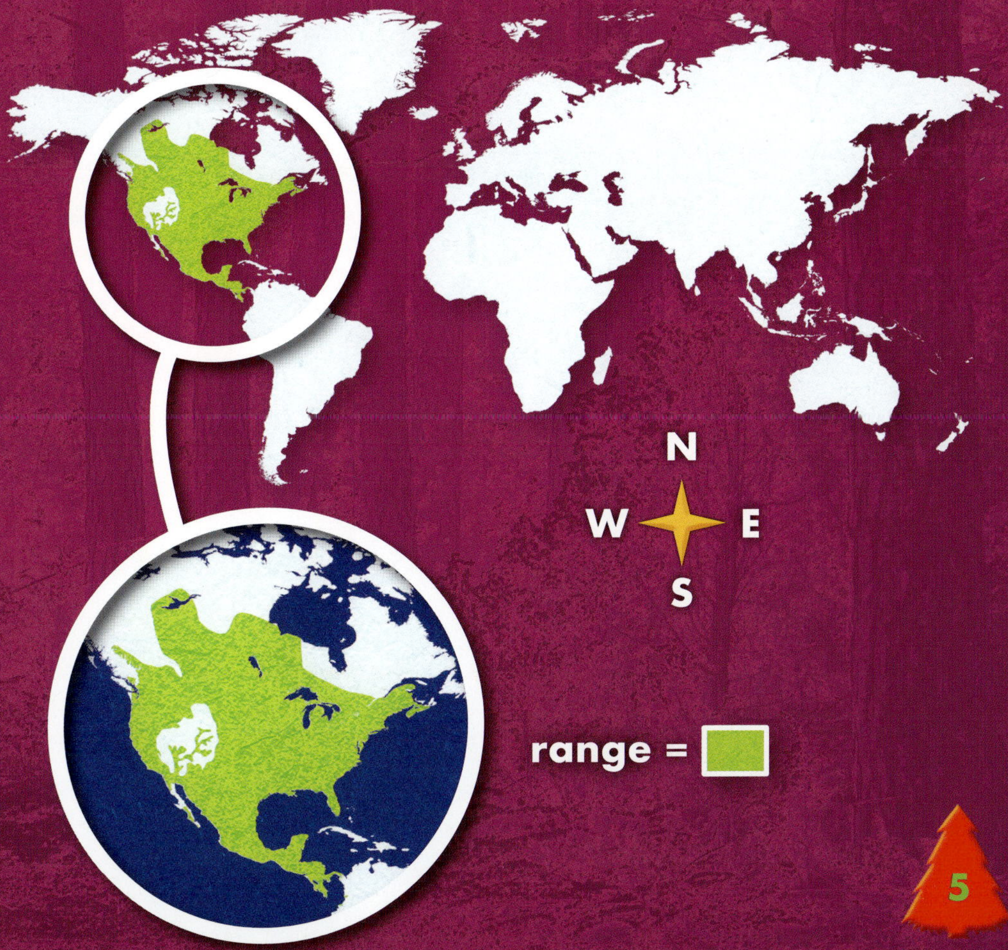

The forest is full of trees. Raccoons are made for climbing them!

Their front paws have five
fingers with sharp claws.
They easily grab branches.

Raccoons can scurry down trees headfirst! Their back feet **rotate** to help them climb up and down.

Speedy climbing helps raccoons escape **predators**.

Special Adaptations

Raccoons have thick, warm fur. The dull color offers **camouflage**.

Raccoons also have black masks. These may protect from the sun. They may also help raccoons spot their friends!

Tree Houses

Raccoons make **dens** in small spaces such as trees and logs. Dens keep raccoons safe from predators.

Dens also keep raccoons warm during winter.

Raccoons must hide quickly from predators. They run up trees to escape coyotes and wolves!

They can also escape to water. Raccoons are good swimmers!

Northern Raccoon Stats

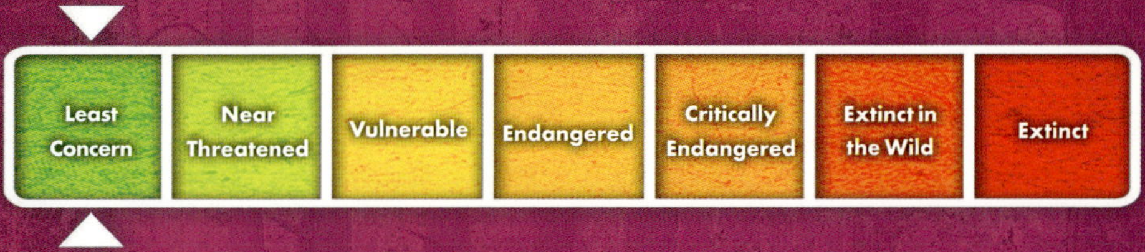

conservation status: least concern

life span: up to 3 years

Midnight Snacking

Raccoons are **omnivores**. They eat small **rodents** and many kinds of fruits and nuts.

They are also **nocturnal**. They look for food at night.

Raccoons often dunk food in water.

Water makes raccoon paws very **sensitive**. They know more about their food if it is wet!

Raccoon Diet

acorns

corn

deer mice

Some raccoons live in cities. They often dig in garbage cans.

These forest critters can find food almost anywhere!

Glossary

adapted—changed over a long period of time

biome—a large area with certain plants, animals, and weather

camouflage—coloring or markings that make animals look like their surroundings

dens—sheltered places

mammals—warm-blooded animals that have backbones and feed their young milk

nocturnal—active at night

omnivores—animals that eat both plants and animals

predators—animals that hunt other animals for food

rodents—small animals that gnaw on their food; mice, rats, and squirrels are all rodents.

rotate—to turn around

sensitive—able to take in a lot of information

thrive—to grow well

To Learn More

AT THE LIBRARY

Petrillo, Lisa. *All About North American Raccoons.* Hallandale, Fla.: EZ Readers, 2019.

Riggs, Kate. *Raccoons.* Mankato, Minn.: Creative Education, 2017.

Storm, Marysa. *Raccoons.* Mankato, Minn.: Amicus, 2018.

ON THE WEB

FACTSURFER

Factsurfer.com gives you a safe, fun way to find more information.

1. Go to www.factsurfer.com.
2. Enter "raccoons" into the search box and click 🔍.
3. Select your book cover to see a list of related web sites.

Index

The images in this book are reproduced through the courtesy of: Romrodphoto, front cover (background); Arto Hakola, front cover (alligator); Orhan Cam, p. 4; Passion4nature, p. 6; Saddako, p. 7; Jennifer White Maxwell, p. 8; Fernando Cortes, p. 9 (top); tome213, p. 9 (bottom); Shooty Photography, p. 10; clayton harrison, p. 11; Zen Rial/ Getty Images, p. 12; Richard Ellis/ Alamy, p. 13; evelyng23, p. 14; Tony Craddock, p. 15; J.A. Dunbar, p. 16; Colin Pickett/ Alamy, p. 17; tswinner, p. 18; Andy Lidstone, p. 19 (top left); Thomas Barrat, p. 19 (top right); Podolnaya Elena, p. 19 (bottom); KristyLouCreative, p. 20; John Cawthron, p. 21; IndiaO, p. 23.